Things That Go Bump....

IN THE NIGHT"!

By Simone Padur

Published by Big Country Publishing

Things That Go Bump In The Night
©2012 Simone Padur
Library of Congress Control Number: 20112012933624

ISBN: 978-0-9847831-7-5

First Edition

Published By
Big Country Publishing, LLC
7691 Shaffer Parkway, Suite C
Littleton, CO 80127
www.bigcountrypublishing.com

The paintings in this book were done in watercolor pencil
ink and photoshop.

Dedicated to my parents for their enthusiasm and inspiration, Shannon O'Hara, Gary Douglas, and his Access Consciousness™ team for giving me the tools to make this possible.

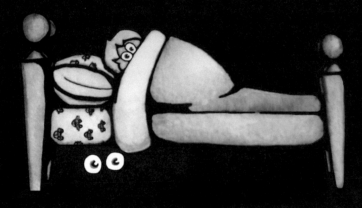

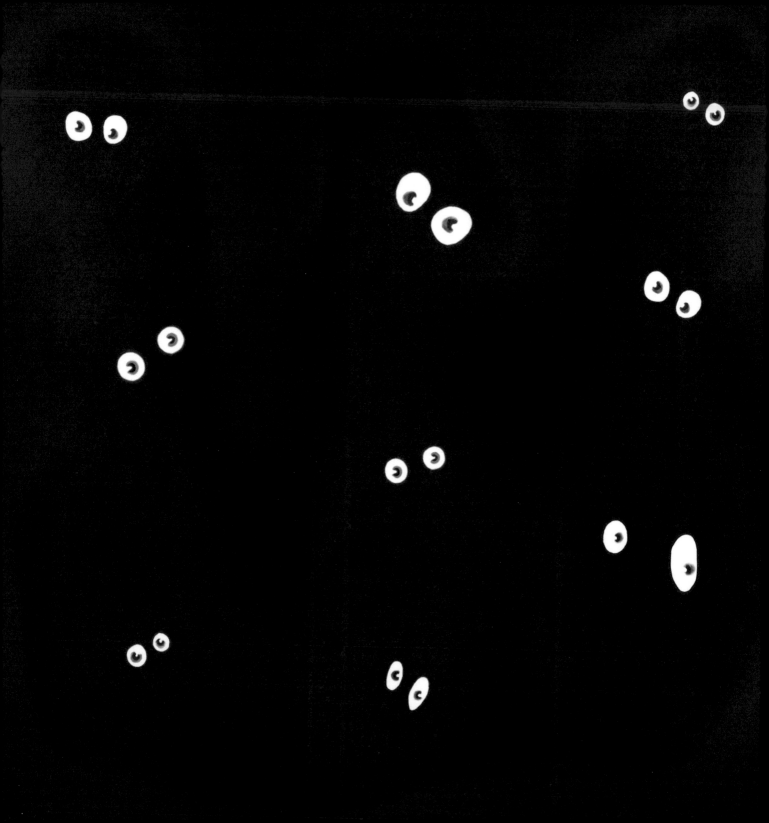

This is a story of a small boy named Sam.

Who heard things that go bump in the night.

He would lie in his bed.

Him and his teddy tucked up tight.

Waiting for his mother to turn out the light and worried about the things that go bump in the night.

He
could
hear them
Lurking under the stairs.

He could
sense them
shuffling behind
Dad's chair.

He could feel them behind the toilet uttering a snore.

He knew it was them peering out the closet door

He hid under the covers.

He sang really loud!

He left on the light.

He counted sheep
till he could count no more.

Then he knew!

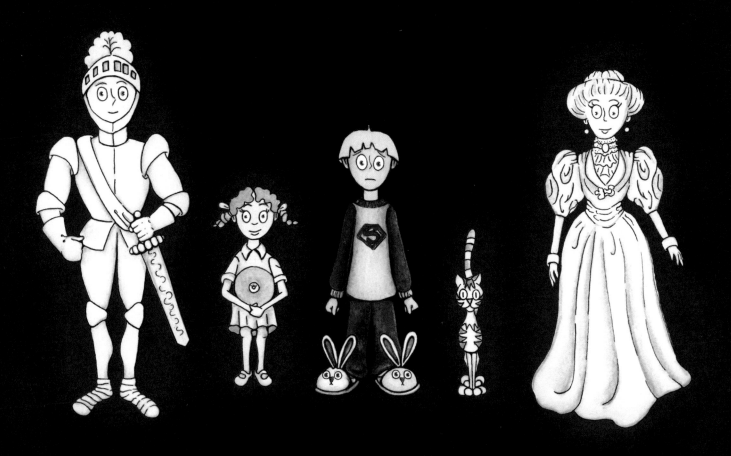

They were beings young and old, short and tall,

from near and far.

There was no reason

to be scared at all.

Sometimes even

Granny came to call.

They can show up in the night and in the day.

They may be tricky and try to get their way.

Hey Sam. What can you do? What can you say?

Ask "TRUTH" and all their tricks will go away.

Remember Sam you are in charge.

There is no need to fear.

You can tell them to pack their bags and get out of here.

Hey Sam.

Now that you know there is nothing to fear.

Do they come in at all hours and chat in your ear?

Do they throw a party and destroy your sleep?

Remember you can choose the hours they keep.

One more thing before you close your eyes.

Picture a light an orangey red and indigo blue bright.

Wrap it around you like a great big hug.

Goodnight things that go bump in the night.

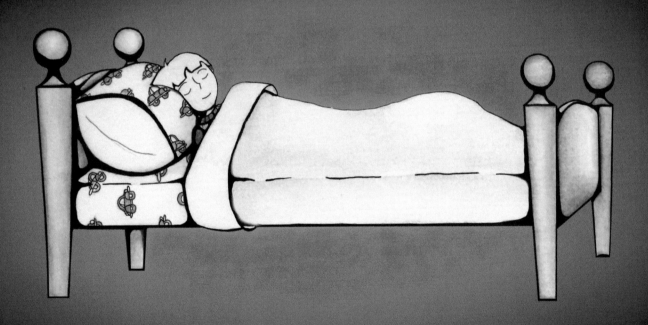

The End

Simone Padur has been teaching children art, drama and storytelling in summer camps and international schools for eight years. She has found that she was constantly using stories in her camp programs and her classes. However, when she went to write them down or draw them they would disapear. Then she started using the tools of Access Consciousness ™ which encouraged her to ask questions of her self and everything around her. Knowing that asking a question would create an awareness she asked: "What kind of book did I require as a child?" Immediately she remembered how terrified she had been of the dark, even into adulthood. With the tools of Access Consciousness ™ she no longer was afraid, and with these same tools of asking questions she had the book outline.

How does it get better than that? What else is possible?

It is with great pleasure that she launches this book into the world for kids young and old.

CPSIA information can be obtained
at www.ICGtesting.com
Printed in the USA
LVIC042043240612

287457LV00002B